To Rory

Hope you l,___ ___ ____

Rowan + Jake

THE KNIGHTS OF PEGASUS

By

IAN MILLER

About the Author

IAN MILLER is one of the most well-kent faces in the West of Scotland.
A man of the cloth. An entertainer. A man who welcomed all denominations, anytime. A man who has married, christened and buried the great the good and the lowly with equal gravitas and humanity....
Ian has also served as a school chaplain for many years and is always a big hit with kids and teachers alike.
The Knights of Pegasus is his first children's title.
His autobiography '*From Habbie to Jeely-Eater*' is available at www.neetahbooks.com

Introduction

'What did you do in the war Daddy?' That used to be question that appeared in stories when I was growing up. In years to come it might be – 'What did you do during Lockdown when Covid 19 knocked on our doors?'

For many the change was very challenging, Jobs were at risk, health was at risk. The education of our children was at risk. If you had any underlying health issue or if you were over 70 there was the prospect of living like a hermit. But maybe, as in the war most of us coped.

Joan and I found we walked more, talked more and I think we laughed more. There were, however, the downsides. In one eight-week period, I found myself conducting 67 funerals. I was unable to visit the bereaved and funerals were conducted with the very minimum of mourners. I found that hard.

Aware that my four grandchildren Ben, Josh, Rowan and Jake would be off school and that as grandparents we would be prevented from offering any kind of support I began to worry how their parents would cope!!! So, I decided I would write a story, a fantasy, which their parents could read to them at bedtime. I don't think it really worked out that way. The children managed to get an extension to bed time and probably by the time their parents had got them to bed... settling down with a glass of wine was perhaps more attractive than reading a story. But eventually they did hear that story... because it was all about them.

They are all different and hopefully the things that make them different will emerge in the story. Though different they are dearly loved. They have all brought so much joy to us. Living close at hand we see a lot of them and that is one of our biggest pleasures. So, I dedicate this book to them To Ben, To Josh, To Rowan and to Jake but also to their parents Derek and Natalie and to Andy and Andrea who have allowed us the privilege of sharing their children with us. You have given us the greatest gift possible.

I hope all who read this will enjoy the story and hopefully I will have captured in this fantasy something that makes those four so special.

Thanks

As always to Paul Murdoch who thought that what started as an intention to amuse four children might be worthy of a bigger audience.

To Ruth, his daughter, who produced the art work. Thanks, Ruth and best wishes as you pursue your studies at the Royal Conservatoire.

To Douglas Campbell - grandfather to Ben and Josh and a former journalist who scanned the script and made some appreciated corrections.

To Joan just frankly for putting up with me and accepting that for me retirement was never going to be 'normal'.

To David Upton and Tony Farrell who promised not to sue me and of course Ross Priory which is our 'escape'.

To Christie Park School, Cardross School and The Vale of Leven Academy for educating our grandchildren. Any profit from the book will be split between them.

And as always to the Vale of Leven community which has been our home for 45 wonderful years. We love the people and we love the place.

Publication of this book was made possible by the generosity of various well-wishers and friends...

The Kinloch family in memory of their parents Ronnie and Jennifer Kinloch of Cardross whose grandchildren Alex, Robbie, Jack, Ella, Hope, Molly and Ava brought them so much pleasure.

Ian McMurdo (ex Director of Education in West Dumbarton) in memory of his wife Nan whose grandchildren Anna, Lucie and Joe were the love of her life

And Joan whose grandchildren Ben, Josh, Rowan and Jake are featured in the story and add so much love and laughter to her life.

Thanks to all the staff at Ross Priory which features greatly in the story, you all have that wonderful ability to always make us feel welcome. You are special to us

Chapter One

Rowan burst into Jake's room. Her brother was playing Fornite on his computer. "You will never guess what has just happened to me?" she said excitedly.

Jake's eyes never left his game.

"Jake" said Rowan, "I sometimes think if a bomb went off in the kitchen or the roof fell in you would just sit there playing that game. DO YOU HEAR ME?" she shouted.

Jake turned around. He looked exasperated. "What is it Rowan? I am playing my game," he barked.

"I can see that, but I have something to tell you." Jake turned again to his game.

"Don't even think of playing that game while I am speaking to you." There was a determination in Rowan's voice her brother was not used to.

He thought to himself, *sisters can be such a pain* but said, "OK Rowan. What do you want to tell me? What has been so exciting, so important, you just must tell me right now?"

She began her story, stating she had been down in the field with Gypsy, her horse. They had been exercising, when, according to Rowan, Gypsy had...SPOKEN to her.

Jake exploded with laughter but, looking at his sister's face, he realised she was being serious. Should he shout for their mum and dad? But, he wondered, how do you tell your parents that your sister has lost the plot?

So, he took a deep breath and said. "Great Rowan, a talking horse. Sometimes, dear sister, I worry about you. Have you been eating too much chocolate again? You know it makes you hyper. It effects your wee brain... Gives you a rush, makes you see things too by the sounds of it. He rolled back on his bed and laughed at his joke. He was about to return to his game wondering what she might come up with next.

Rowan just stood, the look on her face telling Jake she was not amused. There was a silence in the room, then Rowan continued with her story, determined to convince her brother she was serious.

She maintained that, unbelievable though it seemed, the horse HAD spoken to her. There was just the two of them in the field. Rowan had been chatting to the animal as she always did, calling Gypsy by her name. Jake had always thought that was a bit silly.

He thought Gypsy had no idea what her name was. But, according to Rowan, the horse had spoken and indicated Gypsy was the name given to her but it was not her real name.

Her real name was 'Pegasus'.

Jake thought that was a silly name for a horse. He should have kept his thoughts to himself but, being Jake, he didn't.

He just indicated he was going back to his game and told his sister she should not bother him again with silly stories.

Rowan stormed out of the room and slammed the door.

Jake returned to his game wondering how his sister, who usually seemed normal, could think a horse would talk to her and thought no more about it.

During the evening meal, Rowan was strangely quiet. When she eventually left the table, she went straight to her room.

Jake thought that was strange. Feeling a little guilty that he had made fun of her, he shouted: "Rowan, come on down and we can watch Jumanji!". There was no answer. Maybe she did not hear him. Jake went up to her room and knocked on the door. Again, no answer.

Carefully, he opened the door. The girl was sitting on the floor playing with Lego and didn't turn around. Jake sat beside her and asked, "What's the matter Rowan?"

She turned, looked at him, then said: "You know what the problem is. I tell you something and you just dismiss it. You don't ask any questions. You don't try to understand. I know it sounds crazy- but it happened"

Turning back to her Lego she challenged him. "The ball is in your court. You can come down to the field and I will prove it to you. That is the only way you will know the truth."

Later that night, while their mum and dad were watching television, Rowan and Jake decided to sneak out to the field where Gypsy was kept, 100 yards down the quiet country road from where they lived.

The pair climbed the gate and Gypsy came trotting over to them. She nuzzled into Rowan, who clapped her but Jake stood back, determined to put an end to his sister's stupidity.

"Gypsy, what is your name?" said Rowan. The animal made the usual horsey-type sound.

Jake laughed, contempt on his face. "Is that *it* Rowan?" he said. "We have come down here and listened to the only sound a horse is capable of making. Let there be an end to this nonsense. Speaking horse? Rubbish!"

He made his way back to the house, while Rowan looked at the ground, disappointed with maybe just a little tear in her eye.

The horse slowly turned and began to make her way back to the other horses in the field when Rowan looked up and said, "Gypsy, Jake is my brother. He can be trusted. Tell him, just as you told me, what is your real name?"

The horse stopped, its tail swishing. Jake too stopped, a smile on his face. What was his sister on about?

Rowan, Jake believed, was always right. Well this time she was wrong. This time she looked stupid. He moved back towards the house, his lips curled into the smile of boy who knows he has put his sister in her place.

He also knew that, through time, he would remind her of this moment. However, those thoughts evaporated when he heard the name "Pegasus" uttered. He heard it clearly. It was a low rumble but he heard it.

It was not Rowan speaking, it was not him speaking. Slowly he turned around. There was no other explanation. It had to be the horse. His mouth sagged open. Then suddenly, Gypsy or Pegasus, whatever her name, tossed her head and galloped off to join her friends.

Chapter Two

It was a different boy who walked back to the house. He was silent. Still questioning himself, and still confused by what he had heard. It was impossible, but against all logic, he had to admit it - The horse had spoken.

But now, Rowan was full of adrenalin. She would not stop talking. Excitement bubbling over she said, hardly pausing to catch breath. "I told you, Jake. You would not believe me. Gypsy talks. What are we going to do? What does all this mean? Will people come and want to hear her? Will she be on television?"

Rowan paused as if the reality of it all had suddenly hit her and almost despondently said: "Will this mean we will lose her? Will they take her away? Oh, I don't know. We must tell mum and dad."

With all of this going on, Jake had said nothing. He stopped, as if needing time to think.

Looking up at the house, through the trees he could see the lights were on. Then he heard a door opening and his dad shouting... "Rowan, Jake, where are you? It's getting dark. Time you were in".

"We' re coming," they shouted back.

"Rowan," said Jake, "you don't often listen to me but listen this time. Don't tell mum and dad. Let's think about this first. Please."

Again, their father's voice rang out, this time more urgently.

"Rowan and Jake get in here **now**!"

They ran up to their house, passing the stables with Rowan simply saying, "Ok, Jake. I will say nothing but we must talk together, alone."

So later that night, when the pair should have been tucked up in bed, Jake crept out of his room and gently opened the door of his sister's room.

He sat on the edge of her bed.

She put down her book and looked at him.

"Well, brother, what are your thoughts?" she asked.

Jake sighed and said, "Parents can be unpredictable. Dad is not really a 'horse lover'. He puts up with them, Rowan, because of you."

"And mum?" said Rowan. "What would she say?

"I don't know" said Jake. "Mum is not stupid but I think she would be powerless to stop the television and the newspapers coming to Kirkton Byre." (that was the name of their house)

"What I think……" he said pausing for effect.

Oh, my goodness, Rowan thought. *He loves this. He can see himself stepping into Nicola Sturgeon's shoes as first minister of Scotland.*

Then, after a long pause, he said "I think we should talk to our cousins, Ben and Josh."

Rowan was not so sure but then Jake said, "Remember all the adventures we have had together. It would be worthwhile talking to them."

Rowan slowly nodded her head. "Okay, let's talk to Ben and Josh," she said. "Between the four of us, we will know what is right and what we must do with Gypsy... sorry, Pegasus."

The following day, Rowan picked up her phone and pressed Ben's number. He answered, which was a surprise. This was not normal, she usually had to leave a message for him to phone back. But he had recognised her number. Ben spoke in a very plummy, upper-crust accent. *Him and his accents* she thought.

"You are through to the Vale of Leven Medical Practice... Doctor Benjamin Miller here, please leave a detailed message of what is ailing you and, if I feel like it, I will return your call."

"Ben,", said Rowan. "Stop your nonsense. This is serious".

The voice at the other end said: "What ails you child? Speak now or forever hold your peace."

"Ben," she said in exasperation.

"Sorry Rowan. You know what I am like".

He was back to his normal voice and something was on his mind.

"I have just auditioned for a part in the Sound of Music... Friedrich, the oldest of the boys. I'm excited about it and have been trying out accents. Do you want to hear the one I have settled on?"

It was just so like him. He always had to have something on the go, whether music or drama, she thought. Rowan said: "No thanks. That is great news about the Sound of Music but what I am about to tell you will astonish you."

Was he now all ears or was he preparing another smart reply? "However," she continued, "I don't want to speak about it over the phone but you are all coming over to us tomorrow.

"Okay. We'll make an excuse to get away from the adults and talk," Ben said. "I can't wait."

Was he being sarcastic? Sometimes with Ben you couldn't tell.

As she ended the phone call, Rowan said, "Ben, will you please tell Josh?" Ben agreed, and with that she finished the call and began to wonder how she would convince her two older cousins to take her seriously.

Chapter Three

Ben put his phone down and walked over to Josh's room. He knocked on the door and went in. "Josh," he said "That was Rowan on the phone. Apparently, we are going over there tomorrow and she says that she has something exciting to tell us."

"Why didn't she just tell you on the phone?" said Josh, his eyes never wavering from the football game he was playing on the X-Box. It was as if his life depended on it. He viewed any distraction, especially from his elder brother, as unwelcome.

"I don't know," said Ben, "She just said - could we get together. She had something very exciting to tell us. I think her mum was around and maybe she did not want to say more."

Josh didn't answer.

Ben shrugged and left him to his game.

The following day, Ben and Josh, with their parents (Derek and Natalie) left their home in Balloch to drive to Cardross to see their cousins.

Ben looked at the sheep on the hills, and watched the local model aircraft club staging aerial dog fights in the summer sun but all of the time quietly wondering what was so exciting that Rowan was unwilling to share it over the phone? It all sounded so mysterious.

Josh, however, had other thoughts. He did not spare the sheep or the planes a second glance. He was quietly thinking - *I could be playing football.* He had withdrawal symptoms if he and his football were parted.

Soon they were making their way up the driveway to Kirkton Byre.

Josh and Jake were immediately kicking a ball around the small football pitch in the garden. Rowan was quick to get a hold of Ben and suggested, as the adults made their way inside, that they should all take the opportunity to talk. "Just follow me," she said. "I will talk while we are walking."

Jake and Josh's faces were sullen as they reluctantly followed, leaving behind their football game. Josh was still holding the ball.

Rowan began to tell her story. It was obvious Ben and Josh, as they listened, were not going to take her seriously.

Meanwhile, Ben was wondering whether the talking horse knew who would win the next Grand National.

With a giggle, Josh said, "If it can talk, can it play football?"

Jake sniggered, probably quite pleased that no-one was taking his big sister seriously.

Throwing her hair back, she turned on her brother, her eyes flashing. "Jake, you heard it", she said. "You know Gypsy can talk, so stop being stupid."

Josh winked at Jake and Jake managed to supress a smile.

Ben decided that, as the big cousin, the sensible cousin, (which was not always like him) he would take charge.

"Ok Rowan," he said. "Tell us again . . . It's a pretty tall story."

By this time, they were looking over the gate into the field.

Rowan shouted to her horse.

Gypsy looked up, but continued to eat grass.

The second call was more urgent and Gypsy trotted over to where all four children were standing.

Rowan took charge. "Gypsy!" She paused. "Please just speak to us."

Gypsy shied away and uttered that distinctive horsey sound that always sounded like NAAAAY.

Rowan persisted. "Gypsy, speak to us" Ben and Josh are our cousins. You can trust them, tell them your name, your real name."

They waited with bated breath, and in a very measured tone, very clearly Gypsy said, "Pegasus."

Ben and Josh staggered back in amazement. Ben was speechless, which was unusual, and Josh dropped his ball which was even more unusual.

As they stood, open mouthed, the football trickled down the road. For once, Josh's eye was not on the ball.

Gypsy stood motionless, staring at them with her big brown eyes. Blinking now and again to chase away flies, it was as if she was waiting for them to say something and eventually Ben did. He was seldom lost for words. He said: "Gypsy, sorry Pegasus... Ah-ha...the winged horse of Greek mythology. You must be a good age. Pardon my scepticism but firstly Pegasus was a stallion and you are a mare. Secondly, Pegasus was white, and allowing for the fact that you have obviously been having a mud bath, you are not! Thirdly... Pegasus could fly. I don't see any evidence of that possibility. But you can speak and I admit that could make you quite a celebrity."

Ben looked at the other three and said, "There could be money in this for all of us. I could buy that 1932 Morris Minor from uncle Jake." (He had his eye on a vintage car owned by his uncle from Kilbarchan).

In his theatrical way, he announced with a flourish: "There are possibilities for all of us, my friends."

All of the time, Gypsy stood silent and still. Then she spoke and simply said, "This must remain a secret. I can work with you if I decide you can be trusted. It is up to you. Keep my secret and you will benefit. Break my trust and you will look foolish. After all, who will believe a bunch of kids who claim they've heard a talking horse?" With that, she turned and galloped to the other side of the field.

Slowly and silently they walked back to the house.

Josh, then realising he did not have his football, ran back down the road to pick it up, with Jake following.

Rowan and Ben continued towards the house. Finally, Ben said: "This is too much to take in. Let us all think about what has happened tonight." Rowan stopped, looked at Ben and asked, "What does Gypsy mean when she says, 'We can benefit?'"

"I don't know, but I believe we have to keep this a secret," Ben muttered, "at least for now."

They waited until Josh and Jake had caught up. Rowan urged them to keep what they had witnessed a secret.

"It's hard to keep a secret," said Josh. Jake nodded and Ben said, "I agree with Rowan. I think we must. Gypsy or whatever she calls herself has laid it on the line. Who will believe us? Has there even been a talking horse? You all know the answer."

Josh said, "I think there has been... Gran Joan told us once about Mr Ed... He was a talking horse."

Rowan laughed and said, "Yes Gran Joan told me about Mr Ed as well but it was a children's TV programme." They all laughed and Josh just shrugged.

"Ben is right" said Rowan. "We must say nothing just now."

"So what do we do next?" asked Jake.

Josh had the answer... "Jake there is nothing we can do tonight. Let's go back home. I will be goalie and you can fire some shots in at me."

With that, they were off.

Rowan said to Ben. "I will ask if I can come over and see you tomorrow night. I will tell mum and dad that I am struggling with that new violin piece and you have offered to help."

"They will buy that," said Ben with a laugh. "It's funny how parents are always quick to encourage some things."

Rowan laughed with him and said, "Yes and discourage others..."

Chapter Four

The following night, Rowan and Jake travelled to Balloch. Rowan had convinced her parents Ben was happy to help with her music.

Indeed, Jake offered to take his music as well to show Ben how he was progressing with piano. Of course, he would also want to show Josh how he was progressing with his football.

Not long after they arrived, Ben asked his mum and dad, if they could all walk around to Lomond Shores.

"No way," said mum. "You could not be trusted".

"I promise" said Ben…. "There will be no carry on, no running about… Lomond Shores and back. Thirty minutes I promise."

With reluctance, Natalie agreed. So, Ben's parents settled down with Andy and Andrea.

They smiled as the children took off... wondering why they seemed so serious but soon dismissed any real concern. Probably G and Ts, a can of beer and an orange juice for the designated driver helped.

"I still think we should tell," said Jake.

Josh agreed.

Rowan said, thoughtfully, "I know this sounds daft but," she paused wondering what sort of reaction she might get, "I think we should ask Gypsy or Pegasus."

The other three laughed but then she continued. "She did say she might be able to help us. We can at least ask what she meant... I mean, how could she could help *us*?"

Ben said, "Rowan you are right, she did say that. Maybe she'll help me get that 1932 Morris minor or help me to play the Moonlight Sonata or..."

"Yes Ben, we hear you-" but before she could say anything else, Josh was chiming in that Gypsy might help him to become the captain of Partick Thistle.

Jake opened his mouth to say what he was hoping for but was silenced by his sister.

"Enough," she said.

The other three fell silent. By this time, they were at Lomond Shores and they slumped down on one of the benches in the play-park, still wondering what could Gypsy do to help them.

Josh broke the silence when he said, "I think Rowan is right. Let's ask her. Let's ask Gypsy."

The very next day, the four walked down Darleith Road in Cardross and peered over the gate to see where Gypsy was.

She raised her head and trotted towards them and they all jumped over the gate. They walked toward the advancing animal.

Rowan decided to be spokesperson. It was, after all, her horse. "Gypsy...sorry, Pegasus, you said something about helping us?"

Before she could answer, Ben decided to ask his own question. He had been doubting his own sanity. Had he heard the horse speaking, or was it dream? Then again, they couldn't all have had the same dream at the same time. These questions were racing through his head and he felt he had to air his doubts.

"I find it strange to be speaking to you and even expecting an answer, but we all think we heard you. We would love you to help us. You see we all have our dreams. Mine is music, Josh is football, Rowan is horse riding. Jake loves music and football. So, we can come up with loads of things we want to do, but how can you help?"

Gypsy stood still. It even seemed her eyes had stopped blinking, then very clearly she said, "There is no magic trick that can make those dreams come true. Within each of you is something special. Sometimes it takes a while to find out what it is, but when you do, pursue it. Always remember it will take hard work. Just don't give up."

Gypsy paused and added, "Ben, stick in at your music, follow your dream. Rowan, believe in yourself. Josh, I have watched you with that ball...aim for the top. And

Jake…. Ah Jake. You are the youngest. Sometimes you may feel you are not listened to but you are. I will help you, not with your dreams, that's up to you, but I can help you to bring a great gift to others. And I need you to help me?"

"Of course!" they all shouted.

"I want first of all to tell you a little about myself. What I tell you will surprise you, maybe shock you, but I insist it remains a secret. You can never tell anyone."

They all nodded, perhaps a little fearfully wondering what Gypsy was about to tell them.

"How do I start?" mused the horse.

By this time, they had all agreed that when speaking to the horse they would use that name. Josh had fixed on Gypsy's question and answered with his shy smile… "How about - at the beginning."

Ben, of course, had to join in by singing "A very good place to start, are we ready children. Doh a deer…"

The rest shouted, "Ben shut up!" And…strangely, he did.

Chapter Five

So, Gypsy (Pegasus) told the story of how her father was Poseidon, god of the sea and his mother was Medusa the Gorgon. Medusa had been beautiful as a young woman but had been cursed and anyone looking at her turned to stone.

"I think I know her," Ben said: "There a woman just like that in our estate who lives…"

"Be serious Ben", said Rowan.

"So," said Josh, "you weren't very lucky with your parents."

Gypsy simply said, "How true" and continued. "But I was a stunning white horse with wings that meant I could fly. I was very beautiful and my proudest possession was a golden bridle. But that is in the past…. I am more interested in what is happening today."

Jake asked "Can you still fly? Could I jump on your back and could you fly over our school? It's just down the road."

Gypsy answered: "Jake, I can fly and, if you need me to fly, I will fly. We shall see…"

Ben had said nothing so far but chipped in. "Are you trying tell me you have been around for all that time?"

"Yes and No," said Pegasus.

"What kind of an answer is that?" said Rowan.

"I wonder what kind of an answer I can give you that will satisfy you?" said Gypsy.

"In a sense I am immortal and when I die, my soul, the inside bit of me, simply jumps into another foal that is being born at that minute. So, I live on and have been with so many famous horses. You may recognise some of the names."

Josh piped up, "My Grandad Campbell likes horses, racehorses."

"Well he would know some of the names I will mention to you…." said Gypsy and so she did.

"Bucephalus, the horse of the Alexander the Great. Marengo, ridden by Napoleon. Red Rum … a racehorse."

"Grandad would know that one. Sure, he and uncle Chris like going to the races? He once told me... "

"Ssssh," said the rest, interrupting whatever secrets grandad Campbell had told him.

Gypsy continued... "There was Sefton who was blown up by a terrorist bomb. Black Beauty. Trigger. Joey ...."

"Joey?" said Ben, "How do I know that name? Was Joey in the war. Did they make a film about him called Warhorse? I saw it in the theatre. Was that you?"

Gypsy answered, "I was in the real one, Ben, in the first world war, with all the mud and gunfire, men and horses dying together. It was awful. So yes.... I have been around for a long time and I can go forward and backwards in time."

"What do you mean?" asked Rowan. "Are you like Dr Who?"

"Yes Rowan, but I don't really like to time travel and I only do it when I fear that there is no other alternative. However, I feel it may well be necessary very soon and that is why I may need your help," said Gypsy

At that point, a voice rang out. It was Rowan and Jake's dad… "Rowan, Jake, Ben, Josh get up the road…. Where are you?"

"Go," said Gypsy, "Do not keep your parents waiting. You have good parents, all of you. Get back up the road but come back again - the story I have to tell you is not finished."

So off they dashed, running quickly up the driveway, laughing and out of breath.

"Where have you been? "asked dad…

"Talking to the horse," said Rowan.

Their dad made a noise that indicated he was not impressed. "I suppose you're going to tell me that the horse talked back?"

They all laughed. Rowan and Jake linked arms with him and just said, "dad!"

They glanced at each other nervously - *If only he knew….*

Derek and Natalie were a bit amused that their two boys had suddenly developed an interest in horses. They had never been very bothered before. Indeed, Derek had often referred to them as "Big

Dugs' It was almost a family joke. So why the sudden interest in 'Big Dugs'?

They were even more surprised that they knew the name of Rowan's horse and how they were suddenly so keen to go over and see their cousins and walk down to the field.

Natalie had asked Josh what was going on, but Josh had just smiled. He was good at that. He smiled, made a face, and then shrugged his shoulders. So, that wasn't much of a help.

Natalie then spoke to Ben.... He admitted he had never been interested in horses in particular but that all living things interested him. That at least was true.... Bugs, birds, animals... Yes, they could attract his attention.

So, the Balloch Millers found themselves again making the journey over the hill to see the Cardross Millers.

They were welcomed by Andy and Andrea, but were surprised how quickly Ben, Josh, Rowan and Jake rushed down the road to see the horses. *Ah well,* they thought, *it's peace and quiet for us.*

The four arrived at the field.

Gypsy had noticed the car going up Darleith Road and was expecting them. Indeed, her head was leaning on the top bar of the gate, looking over it.

Strangely, it was Jake who spoke up first. "You said you might need us, what did you mean?"

Gypsy's head lifted. She looked one way then another and said, "Can you come over the gate? Let's walk to other end of the field. I have a lot to tell you. I just don't want people to see us together for too long".

And so, they all climbed over the fence and began to walk behind Gypsy. At the far end of the field, furthest from the road, she stopped, turned around and looked at them.

All four stood together. They were excited and just a little uncertain as they wondered if this was the moment when their questions would be answered.

Chapter Six

Gypsy looked at them and paused as if wondering just how much she should tell them. They were after all so young. Could she trust them? Sensing their impatience, she continued - "You asked if I could fly and the answer is yes, but I have to be very careful not to be seen. So, I don't fly a lot, only when it is important."

"How do you know when something is important?" asked Jake.

"Jake," said the horse, "I just know. Maybe some day I will try to tell you and hope you might understand. But can I just ask you to believe me and trust me right now?"

All four nodded.

Josh spoke up. "This thing that might be important, is it to help someone?"

"Yes," was the answer.

Rowan paused then said, "Can we still call you Gypsy? I have known you all this time. Its seems...sort of odd to call you Pegasus."

"Yes," said Gypsy, "I think that is wise, suppose you slip up and call me by some other name then your mum or dad will really be asking questions. You know who I really am, but from now on it is simply GYPSY."

They all smiled. Ben had not spoken but then said, "You confuse me. These flights you talk about, is it some sort of mercy mission? Have I got that right?"

"Pretty much," said Gypsy.

"OK," Ben continued, "I am still confused. When you are on a mercy mission has there been some accident, some catastrophe somewhere and you hear about it? I wont ask right now how you hear. That is a question for later. But let me picture the scene. A few hundred yards from here is the River Clyde. It is big, broad and sometimes it can be quite rough. So, a boat gets into difficulties and suddenly swooping from the sky is YOU. Great! And you rescue all on board. Do they jump on your back? Do you land on the sea or on the deck of the boat? If it's a wee boat your weight would probably sink it. No disrespect intended. If such a thing happened, is it not just possible that a flying horse rescuing stranded seaman from the Clyde would have made the news?"

"Clever boy," said Gypsy. "I thought I could have fooled you all with a simple explanation to satisfy you and gain your trust, but now I need to be very open with you and show how you can be part of that help."

"I am lost," said Josh. "But I am up for an adventure, Gypsy, whatever you are going to do, count me in."

"Me too," said Jake "Can I fly as well?"

Nudging Josh, he said… "That would be brilliant, wouldn't it?"

Josh just smiled.

"There are many ways to help people," answered Gypsy. "I think when I explain it all to you, you will understand what I mean and how I might need you. You will remember I *did* say that I have been the spirit of many great horses in the past. Some you will have heard of, others you will not. Some are well known by boys and girls in other parts of the world but not here in your country. I can still travel to the past but more often than not, I go into the future. I wont take you there right now but I can tell that something is about to happen that will change the way we live and the way we think. Some things we can still change and that is why I need your help. I often use the help of young people because, more often than not, big people don't listen or won't believe, that is why I am asking you."

Rowan looked at the other three and asked, "Are we in? Can we really promise that whatever we are called to do, we will do it? We will trust Gypsy?" Rowan knew and loved her horse. It was easier for her. Perhaps Jake, too, though he was not greatly interested, he would do it for his sister, but what about Ben and Josh?

There was a concern in Josh's eyes, but stepping forward with the same confidence he had when his long stride took him past a line of defenders to slot home yet another goal for his Partick Thistle academy team, Josh took over and simply said, "Gypsy, count us in... All of us."

Ben blinked twice, shook his head, stunned by his younger brother taking 'centre stage' then smiled and he gave a slight nod and said, "Yes Gypsy, count us all in. We are all up for it. We wont let you down."

Gypsy continued with her story. "You must know the world; this planet is facing a huge challenge. You must know about global warming."

"We have been studying that at Christie Park...my school. I know about it," said Josh.

"Also at our school in Cardross," Jake added excitedly.

"Listen," said Gypsy... "Global warming is a serious threat but there is an even greater threat facing the world. I know it is coming. It is in the future but not so very far away. Sadly, people will die. I think you can help me to stop it.

"Is it a war?" asked Jake.

"I suppose it is, in a sense," continued the horse, "But not like a usual war, with bombs and bullets, but a war in which we will all be involved. I have a journey to make. I must go alone. Thank you for your help. Soon we will meet. I will be able to tell you more, and by that time I will know what part you might play, I am asking you to be patient, I hope you understand."

Four heads nodded in unison.

"I will be away for days," said Gypsy, "but it won't seem like that. Have you ever heard of Einstein's theory of Relativity?"

Jake immediately answered. "Yes,"

Gypsy said, "Can you explain it to us."

Jake thought for a few seconds then smugly said, "I know what it is, but it might be too complicated for some of you to understand."

If Gypsy could have smiled she would have. Instead she said, "It's all about time. Mr Einstein once said if you sat on a park bench with a pretty girl for an hour it would seem like a minute. If you sat on a hot stove for a minute that would seem like an hour. Time is strange. Occasionally you think something is taking ages but it is not. Other times it's so quick but its not."

"Yes," said Ben... "When I am in a maths class at school it lasts for ever and yet my music class passes like lightening."

"What I am trying to tell you," continued Gypsy, "is that I will be away for quite a few days, maybe even weeks but it wont seem like that to you. It will be almost as if I have not been away at all. That is time travel."

With a swish of her tail the horse trotted off, leaving four young people looking at each other mystified.

Time travel. Einstein. Relativity. Only *Professor Jake* knew what Gypsy was on about and he was not for telling!

Chapter Seven

Ben and Josh could not wait to return to see their cousins. But it was a few days before mum and dad could be persuaded. When they got there, however, they were met by Rowan and Jake in a state of high excitement.

"Gypsy is back from wherever she was, but as she told us, at no time did she actually seem to be away," said Jake.

Then Rowan chimed in. "Yes. Remember when we last spoke to her? Well, the very next day she was there as usual but she was lying down, she just would not get up to exercise. Mum wanted to call the vet but she seemed OK in every other way. I persuaded mum to wait until the next day and she did."

"Yes," said Jake, "and the next day she was fine but she wouldn't talk to us."

"Jake, she did talk to us," interrupted Rowan, "but she wouldn't say much, just that there was a lot to tell us and that she wanted to wait until we were all together".

"Come on then," said Jake. "Let's go."

The four dashed down to the field, Josh leading the way in his new football boots. They climbed the gate and began rushing to the far side of the paddock where Gypsy was lying down. She must have heard them as she slowly began to get to her feet.

"Gypsy," said Rowan "how are you?"

The horse uttered just one word - "Tired."

"Tell us," said Ben, "What happened? You were only away for one night."

"Relativity, dear Ben, I was away for 10 days in one time zone while you think it was just overnight. I have much to tell. Sit down on the grass and I will let you know what I discovered. I hope you are ready for it. It is in many ways a sad story and a dangerous story and will involve you. When you hear it, if at anytime you want me to stop, just say so. If you don't want to be part of this, just tell me. All I ask is that whatever happens, you keep your promise to keep it a secret."

"You have our promise - and I speak for the four of us," said Ben.

Gypsy told them that after they left, darkness had fallen and the rest of the horses settled down for the night. She said she stood up and walked to the far end of the field and began to stretch her wings.

Jake was curious and immediately wanted to see them. But Josh quickly reminded him that they should do nothing that might attract attention.

Gypsy assured them there would be a right time for them to see her wings and said she was sure that the day would come when all four would fly with her in the biggest adventure of their lives. Josh seemed excited by this prospect and indicated such a day could not come quickly enough.

Ben glanced over at Rowan and, seeing the uncertainty in her eyes, he smiled and gave her a nod of assurance, the way big cousins often do. He also sensed Gypsy's impatience. She had a story to tell and he wanted to hear it.

Almost as if preparing herself, Gypsy paused for a moment and then said, "I took off from Cardross and rising, I turned to take a look at the place I now call home. There was sadness in my heart because I wondered if I might survive the journey. I knew where I was expected to go but was unsure if I would get there or would ever return. So, as I rose into the air, I circled for a while, seeing the outline of the ruins of St Peters College, Darleith Castle, the lights of Greenock, Dumbarton and Helensburgh. As I rose higher I saw the lights of the Vale of Leven and of Balloch, where you live Ben and Josh. I felt sad and a little scared as I prepared to leave the place where I felt safe. However, I had to go because the safety of the world was at stake. Your future Rowan. Yours Jake, yours Ben and Josh. I wondered what would become of you. I thought of the many times I had faced dangers with the children I had chosen to help me. There have been plagues in this world. Disasters, wars and I have been involved in most of them and the outcome has always been good, especially when I have had the help of my chosen children. And you four are the chosen ones."

Chapter Eight

Josh later accused Ben of making a gulping sound which, of course, his brother denied. The four were transfixed and not a word was spoken.

"Maybe one day I will be able to tell you of some of the terrible things I have seen when this is over. However, afterwards it is as if all my memories are erased and I just return to being an ordinary horse again, so just in case that happens again, I want to tell you about some of the things I remember. I was at Dunkirk. I helped wounded soldiers onto the beach as they boarded a little boat called Skylark during the war. I was in France as it happened. I was in London during the terrible Black Death. Oh...one day, I would love to tell you how children from all over the world have helped me. With their help, we have been able to stop disasters, or at least make them not as bad as might have been and that is what I am asking you to do. However, let me return to my story.

I had to force myself to turn from Cardross and fly across the hill. Leaving Loch Lomond behind, I flew across Scotland, crossing the stormy waters of the North Sea, passing over Germany, Switzerland, Austria - too many countries to mention going east all of the time, stopping only now and again to rest and eat. Then, almost half way around the world, I reached my destination."

"Where was that?" asked Ben.

"Ben you must remember as well as flying across countries I was flying forward in time. I eventually stopped in China, in a city called Wuhan, where eleven million people live.

"It was just as the year 2020 started. It was strange to be there. As a horse in the city I would have been exposed to danger. So, I was able to spend some time with a herd of horses on a farm on the outskirts of the city.

The humans were in a state of panic, and I became aware, through their conversation, that a plague was infecting the city."

"Do you speak Chinese?" asked Josh.

"Josh, all language is the same to me. Whatever was happening was serious, very serious...as serious as the plague, Black Death, Cholera, Spanish Flu, Ebola, SARS - and I knew every single one. But what I tell you is so important that you cannot tell anyone. Do you promise?"

Again, there were four very apprehensive nodding heads.

So, Gypsy continued... "This is in the future but not very far away."

"But", said Rowan, "what has something happening in China to do with us?"

"I agree" said Jake and Josh in unison.

Ben thought it appropriate to contribute. "I think I understand. If this is a virus instead of bacteria, it is more difficult to defeat unless there is a vaccine," said the eldest cousin.

"What is a vaccine?" asked Jake.

"Well Jake," said Ben, "It's like something you get when you are a baby, it stops you getting things like measles and mumps. Older people get it too like our grandparents to stop them getting flu".

Josh asked, "Why is there not one of those things... A vaccine... To stop us getting this thing?"

"Because its new, I suspect," said Ben "viruses can also change, making them more difficult to defeat."

Rowan smiled inwardly because all the time Gypsy was nodding her head as Ben spoke. She just said to herself - *and some people think horses are stupid*?

Ben had not finished but he closed by saying, "Those things can spread so quickly, someone who is infected coughs and if you are close enough, you can breathe in the virus and become infected.

"You infect someone else and so on. I think if I touch something, say a car door, and you touch it later the virus can jump onto your hand. You touch your face and it enters your body through your nose, mouth or eyes. That is how it spreads. If it starts jumping from country to country, its called a pandemic." He said all this almost without stopping for breath.

Rowan had been listening to her big cousin with eyes wide open, wondering if that was why you were always told to wash your hands. But instead she asked very simply: "Gypsy are you telling us it might come here?"

"No" said Gypsy. "I am not telling you that... I am telling you it WILL come here."

Chapter Nine

The four were stunned by this news and eventually Josh found his voice and asked, "Will people get ill?"

Gypsy answered in a low voice, "Yes they will."

"How can we beat it then?" asked Jake.

"Before very long you will hear all about it. Very clever people will try to develop a vaccine, but that will take a long time and I will talk to you about that. But I am sure you can help."

The four looked at each other. They were anxious but also excited.

Gypsy continued. "Lots of things will happen and it will be very hard for you. People will be asked to wash their hands a lot, many times a day with soap and warm water and to do it for 20 seconds."

"We wash our hands already," said Rowan. "I know it is important."

Jake asked, "How long is 20 seconds, how will I know when to stop?"

"Well if you sing 'happy birthday' twice, that will take you about 20 seconds", said Jake's sister.

Ben nudged Jake and said, "Just sing it into yourself. I have heard your singing."

Jake nudged him back but knew Ben was kidding.

Ben was often told he washed his hands too much. He thought how much he would enjoy reminding his dad and gran Joan to wash their hands.

"So it's simple," said Rowan, "Wash your hands and you are Ok."

"No," said Gypsy, "There will be much more than that. You will have to stay apart from your friends and other members of the family, even grandparents. It will be hard."

"For you Josh, no more football training with Partick Thistle."

"What?" said Josh. "No that can't happen...never."

"Ben and Jake... No more music lessons. Rowan... No ice skating or horse riding lessons. There is so much you will miss.

Your school show, Hairspray, will be cancelled Ben and you don't know this yet but you were going to be asked to play the part of Friedrich in the Sound of Music at the Kings Theatre. You will go to auditions and come though them and be down to the last one. But then it will be cancelled."

Ben was miffed. "You are kidding. You must be! You are having me on... Really. I would just love to play that part."

"And you will someday", said Gypsy, "but this show will be cancelled and you must say nothing. Your chance will come."

"What is the point of going to the auditions then?' the boy asked.

"You must continue to act as normal, said Gypsy, "Who knows, maybe someone will find a cure, but if you go to the audition and it turns out as I predict, you will know I am telling the truth". The horse added, "There is one other thing.... school will be cancelled too."

"Yes!" Three of them said. Only one remained silent. Rowan liked school.

"Your lives will change and change dramatically and you will have to do what you are told. Don't mix with other people, wash hands regularly and exercise and there's something else..."

"What is that?" asked Jake.

"Please help your mums and dads. This will not be easy for them. You will become bored and when you do, you might get up to no good. Are you listening, Ben? You too, Jake and Josh. Not of course you, Rowan, you are a princess and you will be just perfect!"

The other three laughed.

"I am joking" said Gypsy "but please help your mums and dads. Be good for them. They will be finding it difficult. But it *will* end!" Gypsy continued. "Now for the serious bit. I want to tell you how you can help.

"When I was in China, I managed to speak to some children there. They were scared but I managed to persuade them that I could be trusted. They had a very old great grandfather. He was well over a 100 and believed there was something that could ward off the disease but no-one would listen to him. He told the children of a special plant called Gunnera Manicata.

Josh and Jake giggled thinking what a funny name.

"What are you laughing at?" asked Rowan.

"Jake said, "Josh thinks this Gunnera fellow is the one that Liverpool has just signed."

"Be serious," said Rowan.

"Gunnera Manicata?" Rowan asked, "Have I got that right? So, where can we find it... where does it grow?".

Gypsy answered simply – "Brazil."

"Brazil.... How can we ever get to Brazil?" asked Rowan.

"We can and we will," said Gypsy. Then she paused and said slowly, "We must."

"So tell us a bit more about it?" asked Josh.

"Well Gunnera Manicata looks like a great big rhubarb plant. It was also said to be the food of dinosaurs and it can only be found in Brazil."

A thoughtful smile came over Ben. He turned to others with the knowing look of a magician who is about to pull a rabbit from a hat and said, "Just think guys, a plant that looks like giant rhubarb? Is it just possible that we don't need to go as far as Brazil?"

"What do you mean?", asked Gypsy.

Looking at his three fellow conspirators. Ben smugly said, "A big plant that looks like Rhubarb. I don't think we need to pack our swimming gear to swim on the Copacabana Beach or climb Sugar Loaf mountain or take part in the Mardi Gras celebrations – although that would be wonderful."

Jake said, "All right, Ben, what are you trying to say?"

"Plant that looks like rhubarb. Do I need to spell it out? think!" replied Ben.

Josh's face became suddenly alive. "Ross Priory!" he declared.

"Yes", said Rowan. "That stuff that grows right over by that beautiful circular hole in the wall."

Gypsy was not convinced. "I am listening to you and would love to think it were true but no... I love your enthusiasm and hate to dampen it, but to Brazil we must go."

Josh stepped forward and said, "You have astonished us today, and maybe even frightened us."

Pushing him aside Jake, standing shoulder to shoulder with Josh, said, "We Millers stick together. We have promised to help and we will. If Brazil is where we need to go, so be it."

Rowan looked at Gypsy and just said, "Let us try to prove to you the solution might be much closer. Will you let us try to do that?"

Slowly but reluctantly the horse nodded.

Chapter Ten

Much later, the children hatched a plan that would require secrecy, stealth and persuading Gypsy to fly.

A few days later they were standing in a circle speaking to Gypsy. They explained exactly where the plant was. Although she did not want to dampen their enthusiasm, she was sticking to the old man's story - Brazil was the only place where you could find it.

Rowan tried, after all it was her horse. But Gypsy was unconvinced.

Eventually, Josh said, "The only way to convince you is for us to take you to see the plant. For you to ride there would take quite a few hours travelling over fields and jumping hedges."

"That would attract attention," said Jake.

"It would attract the police," Josh said. "Could you imagine us all on top of Gypsy being stopped on the Gartocharn Road."

"Yes," said Ben, "I can just see it... "Hello, Hello, Hello, what do we have here, three small boys and girl on a runaway horse, I think I will have to breathalyse all of you."

They laughed but were brought back to reality when Gypsy, realising what was in their minds, said, "So you think me flying over the heads of people would not be noticed?"

"It would not," said Josh, "if we did it at night?"

"You have flown at night, haven't you? Surely you can see at night?" asked Jake.

"Of course I can," said Gypsy "but this would be a waste of time. Gunnera Manicata can only be found in Brazil."

"Trust us," said Rowan. "We will do this. It is up to us to find a way to meet you here and to fly to Ross Priory at night."

There was a long pause. Gypsy swished her tail then said, "If that is the only way to prove to you that the plant exists only in Brazil, I will do it."

Ben chipped in, "Our next big problem is somehow persuading our parents that Josh and I can sleep over at Kirkton. That would give us the chance to wait until your parents are in bed and then sneak out. Is that agreed?"

The other three nodded.

Luckily, Jake was having a birthday party in a few days and he and Rowan asked if Ben and Josh could sleep over.

Everything went to plan and when the party ended and Jake's other cousins, William and Jenny, had gone home, Ben and Josh said farewell to their mum and dad and dashed upstairs.

They set alarms to wake themselves at 2.30am and when everything was still and quiet, all four crept down stairs, opened the door, sneaked out, and walked down to the field where Gypsy could be seen in the moonlight.

Rowan had brought the bridle and saddle.

Everyone else stood by as she saddled up then climbed aboard. The other three squeezed on behind her and soon they managed to settle down.

Gypsy, realising she was carrying a precious cargo, stretched her wings. They seemed to appear as if by magic - bright, white and almost shining in the moonlight. She appeared to take a deep breath and then slowly but surely those huge wings began to beat and the horse steadily began to rise.

The passengers clung on, Rowan's arms clasped around Gypsy's neck. Four pair of eyes danced in the moonlight as they realised they were now higher than the house, higher than the trees.

Gypsy turned, making sure the four were safe, and began a slow, steady journey over the fields.

Jake, who was at the back, turned around to see the lights of his house twinkling in the darkness.

Ben spoke into Rowan's ear. "Look Rowan, there is St Peters College, doesn't it look eerie in the moonlight?"

Rowan nodded, perhaps too scared to say anything.

They were still rising, passing over trees and the road Ben and Josh often travelled when visiting them in Cardross.

In the distance, they could see the twinkling lights of Dumbarton. They could even dimly see the outline of Dumbarton Rock as if it was guarding the sleeping town.

As they reached the top of the hill, before the descent to Alexandria, they saw the lights of Bonhill on the other side of the valley, its houses stretching up the hillside. Then they were following the twisting River Leven as they made their way north to Balloch and Loch Lomond.

"Gypsy!" shouted Josh, "Fly over my house, I will point it out to you as we pass!"

And then he saw it, his goal posts in the back garden, his parents unaware of what was passing overhead.

On they flew, above the Maid of the Loch steamer, the last paddle ship to be built.

Would the ship sail again? Perhaps, thought Ben. He pointed down. "When she sails again, I will be on the first voyage."

Rowan was so glad that the moon was shining. It made it easier for her to steer Gypsy to their destination.

Rowan made the decision to take Gypsy up the Loch. In the distance, she could see the lights of the Inchmurrin Hotel. If she were able to fly over the hotel then soon she would see, off to her right, her destination.

All was going well and soon they would see that magnificent building standing proudly near the shore.

As they turned towards Ross Priory, Rowan could see the lights of the avenue leading down to the little Lochside cottage.

She realised they were too high so she urged Gypsy to fly in a wide sweep.

They passed the lodge where the manager, David, slept. He was the man who often told Ben about the ghost of Ross Priory.

What would he make of this?

Turning over the golf course, passing over the road to the Loch Lomond pumping station, Gypsy began to glide.

Looking over Rowan's shoulder, Ben theatrically announced their destination. "Behold, the walled Garden bathed in moonlight!"

From behind him, Josh more realistically said, "Watch out for the greenhouses! We don't want to land on one of them."

However, Rowan had everything under control. Slowly and gently, she ensured Gypsy had landed on the open grass. Jake and Josh jumped off first with Ben and Rowan hot on their tails.

Chapter Eleven

"Did anyone bring a torch?" asked Jake.

"I laid one out, but forgot it," said Josh.

"Blast," said Ben, "I dropped mine coming down the stairs... But wait, I have my phone. That will give us some light if we need it."

Guided by the moonlight, they moved towards a hole in the wall where they could access the plant Gypsy had to see.

"Go on, Rowan. Show Gypsy that Gunnera doesn't only grow in Brazil," said Jake.

Rowan relished the moment. She took Ben's phone and raised the beam to catch the classic outline of the plant that looked so much like a giant Rhubarb plant.

Gypsy was breathing quite heavily after carrying all four of them. She moved forward then stopped quickly.

The animal stared, shook her head in amazement, and then said, "My goodness,

I think you're right. That's it. It's exactly as that old Chinese man described it. There can be no doubt. I knew you could help us. Gypsy blinked her big eyes at Rowan. "I was *meant* to be your horse, Rowan, and you were *meant* to have such a fine brother and two wonderful cousins. We are quite a team and you have saved us a long, dangerous journey to Brazil. This is what we have been looking for. I hope that old gentleman was right. And you have found it so close by. Time is getting on," she added, "We must get back to Cardross. You must get back to your beds before your parents wake. Later, we can decide what we will do with your discovery, but this has been a good night, a very good night's work. Jump up and let's make the journey home."

So, they did, excitedly, while relishing the thought of a nice warm bed to climb back into.

On the way home Josh was scared that Jake might fall off. He was at the back and beginning to nod off. "Jake! Keep your eyes open. It won't be long."

It didn't seem long before they had left Gartocharn behind, taking a short cut over the hills, passing Bonhill Church, right beside the river Leven where their grandfather had been the minister.

Still trying to keep Jake awake, Josh pointed out that Neil McCallum who scored the first goal for Celtic, was buried there.

Jake grunted. "I wish I was home in my bed..."

They realised dawn was breaking and they could see Dumbarton Castle clearly. Then it was down the river Clyde to Cardross and the field, where they landed softly.

Rowan removed the bridle and saddle.

Sleep had almost overtaken Jake so Ben grabbed his hand and hurried him back to the house.

Josh, staying behind, helped Rowan take the bridle and saddle back to the stable and then like the other two they crept up the driveway, into the house.

Mission accomplished.

The next day, Rowan's mum could not get them out of bed. Her dad, suggested a bucket of cold water might be the answer. He even sung at the top of his voice, but apart from a few grunts and a rustling of bed covers no noise came from the four children.

Indeed, it was almost 11am before, one by one, all four made their way down for breakfast.

Rowan was clutching Mash, her stuffed toy Rabbit, under an arm, Jake came down trundling Kwenguin, a stuffed toy penguin, behind him.

It must have been as big as himself, its head bumping off every step as he made his unsteady way to the breakfast table.

Josh carried his 'Wa Wa', a crocheted old cot blanket knitted by his Great Aunt Tiddle; without which he would not, or could not, sleep.

Ben looked as if he did not have the energy to pick anything up though if his cello had been there, it might have been an option.

"Right Guys" said Andy, "What do you want for breakfast?"

"I think I would rather go back to bed, what about you, Jake?" said Josh.

Andy looked puzzled. "Why are you so tired? What were you up to? Did you get up after we went to bed?"

At that moment, the phone rang and Andy went to answer it.

The children looked relieved.

"What are we going to tell him?' asked Rowan.

Blank and sleepy faces looked at her. Obviously, they did not have a clue.
Josh said, "Ben is usually good with excuses. Let him speak for all of us."

Andy finished his telephone conversation and their hopes that he would forget his question were dashed when he said, "OK, so what were you up to last night?"

Taking a deep breath Ben said, "Well you see when you went to bed we got up, crept down to the field saddled up Gypsy and all four of us climbed aboard. And you know what? She took off like an aircraft.

"We flew up to Ross Priory, landed in the walled garden and played a game of hide and seek in the moonlight. It was wonderful and we would like to do it again!"

At that, Andy had heard enough. "Right Ben, no more fairy stories. Rowan and Jake - it will be an early night tonight for you two." He turned to Ben. "And I suspect for you, Ben and Josh, it will be the same. That was your mum and dad asking if we could keep you for a couple of hours. They will pick you up early afternoon."

As Andy walked away he chuckled to himself and simply said, "Weans!"

Chapter Twelve

"Great," said Ben to the others, "Let's all go down the field and see how Gypsy is doing after her night flight. My goodness if Tam o'Shanter's Meg could have flown like Gypsy, Cutty Sark would not have got near her and she would still have her tail."

The other kids looked a bit puzzled as they walked down to see Gypsy. They soon saw that she was waiting for them at the gate.

Rowan was so excited. She wanted to know if they could do it all again?

She babbled away about how she would like to tell her friends at school. No-one would ever have had such exciting things happen to them.

Gypsy looked at her sadly and said, "Rowan, you know you can't. In any case, I think there will be one more flight before this adventure is over."

Jumping up and down they all clamoured, "Where to, Gypsy, tell us, where to?"

"Brazil?" asked Jake.

"No Jake, not Brazil. somewhere much nearer."

"Tell us, tell us!" they shouted.

"I will tell you when you are ready to hear but first there is a task for you all. This is where I need you to do something I can't do. This is your big moment."

"What is it?" they asked.

"I want you to go back up to Ross Priory and cut down some of that big plant we saw."

"The Rhubarb tree?" said Josh.

"Yes, Josh. Cut down maybe two or three stalks. We need the stalks and we need the leaves. In fact, it would be best if we could also get one out by the roots."

"We will try," said Jake.

"What will we do with them?" asked Rowan.

"Just bring them back, hide them somewhere and I will tell you how our story, hopefully, will come to a perfect end."

At that moment, there was a car horn tooting and hands waving out of the window. It was Ben and Josh's mum and dad coming to pick them up. Leaving Gypsy, they ran up the driveway after Natalie's car.

She opened the car door and, smiling, said, "Well what have you been up to?"

Immediately, Ben started, "Well you won't believe this but last night when uncle Andy and auntie Andrea were sleeping, we crept out of the house and…"

His story was interrupted by Rowan, who said, "Right, Ben, you and your tales! Aunt Natalie, we had a great night and great fun!"

"Well", said Derek… "How's about we take you all out somewhere? A park? Or down to Helensburgh for an ice cream?"

In unison they all said, "No. Ross Priory."

"Are you not sick of Ross Priory?" asked Derek.

"No" said Jake… "Who could ever be sick of Ross Priory?"

In any case," said Ben. "I think I would like to have a look at that big Rhubarb-like plant in the walled Garden. I have a biology project to do and it has been suggested that I try to cultivate an exotic plant. I think if we could get a bit of that plant that would be perfect."

"Yes and we can go down to the swings," said Jake and Josh.

"And even play hide and seek!" added Rowan.

Natalie and Derek agreed. Soon they were away back over to Balloch, up to the village of Gartocharn and down Ross Loan to the Priory.

The four children looked at each other, thinking how different it was in the daylight. Ben wanted to go to the garden immediately. The other three wanted to go to the swings.

Ben eventually persuaded his mum and dad to let him go and have a look at the plant and then join them.

His Dad said, "Right Ben, no nonsense, go look and then come down and join us, no digging or hauling things up by the roots."

"Ok", said Ben, "Can I have the car keys in case I bring back just a very small cutting. I will leave it in the boot and join you all."

"OK" said dad. "But lose those keys and you are walking back. Come to think of it, we are all walking back! So, be careful."

Ben nodded then tucked his hands into the pocket of his anorak where no-one could see the little trowel and clippers he had brought with him.

Quickly he raced along the path to the garden entrance via the hole in the wall. He looked up to see if anyone was there and heard a tractor in the distance. Then he heard a chainsaw.

There was no one in the garden so, as quickly as he could he cut away one of the larger stalks then, using his trowel, he dug deep down and managed to extract a smaller yet wholly intact plant.

Then the boy grabbed everything and fled through the large circular hole in the wall just as he heard the garden door banging at the far end.

Ben took a peek and saw Tony, the head gardener, going into the green house. *A narrow escape*, he thought.

Chapter Thirteen

Ben dashed to the car park carrying his precious cargo, then opened the boot and threw everything in. He locked the car and made his way to the Priory to wash his hands.

Just as he emerged, the manger and family friend, David came down the stairs.... "Hi Ben," he shouted. "What are you up to?"

Ben grinned.

"Should I not ask?" Davie continued. "Are you on a ghost hunt?" He made a *woo woooing* sound that any ghost might make. "I saw your mum and dad down at the Lochside. Tell them to come in for a coffee or a beer."

David had filled Ben's head with the stories of the Ross Priory ghost. Somehow the ghost seemed much more believable on a dark and stormy night with wind and rain lashing at the window, lights flickering and floor boards creaking. In the sunshine, it was much easier to dismiss.

Ben made his way down to catch up with the others. As he ran he could hear their cries. By this time Josh and Jake were playing football in the large grassy area in front of the loch, while Rowan was on the swings. Ben joined her and said, quietly, "Job done."

Derek and Natalie were sitting on a bench looking out over the Loch to the islands of Inchcailloch, Inchfad and Inchmoan with a wee part of Inchmurrin also visible.

Ben Lomond stood out clear against the blue sky and they glanced at the Conic Hill and thought of the times they had gone over it on the way to Fort William on the West Highland Way.

Soon the adults decided it was time to get the four children home but not before popping into the Priory for drinks.

As they sat in the lounge, Natalie thought Rowan and Jake were about to fall asleep and Derek wondered exactly what high jinks they had all been up to the night before.

"Right you lot", he said clearing up the glasses and coffee cups. "By the look of you all it's an early night for you... what exactly were you up to last night?"

"Well, dad," said Ben, "we flew up here on a flying horse last night, you would not believe how alert we felt then... The moon was shining and-"

"Aye right. Ben, thank you...let's go."

Three nodding heads dosed in the rear of Natalie's car but one remained awake, his eyes closed.

His challenge was to get the Gunnera plant out of the car and secrete it somewhere at Kirkton without questions being asked as to why a substantial amount of plant life was deposited in the boot.

However, luck was on his side as his mum and dad ensured that the half-asleep Rowan and the comatose Jake were taken to their house while the engine of the Peugeot purred away and the doors were left open.

Ben took his opportunity, left the car, dashed round to the rear, opened the boot and removed all traces of the plant.

He managed to hide it among the trees and bushes that surrounded the house, then returned to the car just as his parents came back. He could see his dad was about to ask a question for which he might not have an answer so he said, "I just needed a wee bit of fresh air, I was nearly asleep...feel better now."

Soon they were home. Josh sort of woke up and made his way sleepily into the house. Ben dashed into the house and ran upstairs ignoring his father's voice as he shouted. "Ben, there is dirt in the boot of this car... Where did that come from?"

He quickly shut the door of his bedroom and began to attend to his bonsai plants. A few days later, the intrepid four were back together again, examining the hidden Gunnera Manicata plant before they went down to speak to Gypsy. It was then they found her plan was now hatched.

"Tonight you must be ready," she said, "All of you. There will be suspicion if Ben and Josh ask for another sleep over at Kirkton. So, this is what we will do.

We are coming to the end of our adventure but this is the most difficult and dangerous part. After tea we must make a journey. It's not a long journey but we will have to go forward in time. The one benefit is that when we do so, it will appear as if you have not been away for any time at all."

"What?" asked Ben.

"I don't expect you to understand but trust me. The second thing is that there is an element of danger. We might not return we might get locked into the future."

"Does that mean we won't see mum and dad again?" asked Rowan.

"No," said Gypsy. "When we go into the future it may mean we remain there for a while. In this case, it's no big deal.

"We are only going to go six months or so into the future so the worst will be that you lose six months of your lives."

"Will I miss the football season?", asked Josh.

"Will l miss six months of school?" asked Jake.

"Yes you will but you wont know it," answered Gypsy.

Josh pondered the loss of even part of the season, how would he cope, but then with reluctance said, "OK, let's go."

"Rowan and Jake, having eaten your evening meal you will come down to the field, bringing the saddle and bridle. Say to mum and dad that you are only going to be about five minutes, that is all it will seem to them. You will then both climb on and we will pick up Ben and Josh," said Gypsy.

"But won't we be seen?" asked Rowan. "You have always been worried about being seen."

"No," said Gypsy, "when we travel through time we will be invisible. The only issue will be at the beginning when we pick up Ben and Josh. Their mum and dad can't see them leaving because for an instant they will disappear only to return seconds later so they must not see you going."

Josh had the answer. "He turned to Ben and said, "you should ask to go down and cut Gran Joan's grass and I can offer to come down and pick up the bits.

"Gran Joan just lets you get on with it and Gum (their nickname for their grandfather) will be in that wee office of his. He will see nothing."

"That would work," said Gypsy. If she could have smiled she would have.

Chapter Fourteen

In the early evening, all four did as they were asked.

Jake, Rowan and Gypsy left Cardross and it seemed, as if in an instant, that they were picking up Ben and Josh at Gran Joan's house in Alexandria.

They held on tightly. With the wind whistling through their hair, they were unable to see anything, it was like being in an aircraft above the clouds, unaware of speed or time.

In what seemed just a few minutes the light had gone and they were aware of falling out of the sky, still clinging to Gypsy and landing on an open stretch of grass. They could see, a few hundred yards away, a very large house, more like a castle.

Dogs were heard barking as they scurried around the feet of a woman who had just emerged from the front door of the building into a little covered porch.

Then she began to walk, leaving the light behind and the dogs followed, yelping and barking as they scampered into the darkness.

"Who is she?" asked Rowan.

"You will soon know. Did you recognise the dogs?" said Gypsy.

"How would we recognise the dogs?" asked Ben.

"They are corgis, does that give you a clue?"

"No!" gasped Ben. "You must be kidding, it cant be....."

Suddenly, out of the darkness, came the scampering corgis followed by their mistress.

The four children retreated into the darkness, while the woman. spotting the horse, came over, and began to pat Gypsy....

"Well now, what are you doing here?" she asked.

She staggered back when Gypsy said, "Good to see you, Maam."

"Did you just speak?" she asked. "Horses don't speak. I have known them all of my life, ridden them, loved them. She rubbed her ears, doubting herself.

"Maam you are right. They don't. But as you know they are very intelligent and I have been given this gift, plus many others, too numerous to mention, which would stagger you.

"However, tonight all I can say is that I am only allowed to speak if I can, in some way, use my gift to help the world, and that is why we are here tonight."

"What?" exclaimed the lady. "There are more of you?" Her initial surprise was replaced by curiosity. "How did they get here?" she said, suddenly aware of the children. "How were they not stopped by security?"

Ben, Josh, Rowan and Jake emerged from the shadows, Rowan delivering a most beautiful curtsy.

"My goodness," said the lady. "Do your parents know you are here?" She looked around wondering if others had also evaded her guard's scrutiny.

"Maam," said Gypsy, "have you heard of William Shakespeare?"

"Of course I have," she said, sounding a little annoyed that a horse should ask such an impertinent question.

"Then you will remember what Hamlet said to his friend Horatio," continued Gypsy.

"There are more things in heaven and on earth than are dreamt of in your philosophy," said the lady.

"So," continued Gypsy, "can you, just for a minute, trust us and listen as we explain why we are here?"

She nodded and motioned Gypsy to continue.

"One of the gifts I have been given is to travel into the future and I know that sometime, probably quite soon, there will be a virus which will spread over the world and even arrive here in Scotland.

"I don't expect you to believe me. I mean, if someone told you yesterday that you would meet a talking horse would you have believed them?"

"Well..."

"Would you believe that a horse and four children could evade the security of this place?"

"Probably not," she mused.

"Here is what we would like to ask you to do," said Gypsy. "You will watch the news as I know you do. You will follow what is happening in other parts of the world and when you hear of a virus that is spreading in China you will know that we are telling you the truth."

The lady looked puzzled.

"I can even tell you where in China. It will be in a city called Wuhan. I have been there I have seen what it can do. Maam," pressed Gypsy, "many people, the people you try to serve will be affected and it will be a long time before a vaccine can be found or a treatment discovered to make people well."

"That sounds terrible," said the lady.

"You were a young woman during the war. I know your memories are vivid of that time," said Gypsy, "and the times ahead may be just as difficult for a while for your country. But believe me. I met an old man near Wuhan who was convinced there is a remedy that can be extracted from a plant called Gunnera Manicata."

"Really?" said the lady.

"We have brought some to you," said Gypsy, "the children have it. Can you find a way to plant some of it, and with your resources try to keep it alive and well?"

The lady said: "I just can't believe what I am hearing. A talking horse, indeed a flying horse. What is your name?"

The children realised that there was the risk of Gypsy starting off on the whole Pegasus story. It was hard enough to convince the lady that what they were telling her was true without involving a Greek legend, so they answered quickly in unison. "GYPSY!"

"Well, Gypsy," she said, "You can't expect me to take in all of this but I will be watching and at the first sign of the prophecy you have made coming true I will speak to people who will investigate your claims.

"If the threat is a serious as you believe it to be, we will owe you a great deal."

Hearing this, Rowan was scared that Ben might try to strike a deal for her to buy the 1932 car from his uncle so she quickly said, "Maam, for us to have helped others would be all that is important."

Josh looked at Jake, who looked at Josh both thinking they might have tried for a better deal.

Without another word the lady looked around, realising the corgis had been silent. They, too, seemed to have been struck dumb by the talking horse. She then turned to the children and said, "So now tell me, what part did you play in all of this?"

"Well," said Rowan. "Gypsy is my horse."

"Really," the lady said as she smiled. Later they were all to agree that she had a lovely smile.

Gum had often told them that. He would love to hear this story but of course he never would.

Chapter Fifteen

Gypsy had spoken but Ben was anxious for the lady to know the part they had all played. "Well Maam," he began, having now realised who the lady was. "Gypsy told us of the old man she met in Wuhan and how he believed this plant, Gunnera Manicata, had healing properties... Well, he also stated that the plant could only be found in Brazil."

All of the time, Jake was keen to contribute so he said, "But we knew that near our house, close to Loch Lomond, there was a walled garden where it grew".

"But we also knew", said Rowan, "that being a horse, Gypsy could not dig it up so we did that."

Before Josh could speak, Ben was determined he would have the last word and ensure that the lady was clear about what they were asking.

So he said, "I suppose that is about it, not very much I suppose but we have brought it to you. We would ask that you plant the one with the roots and perhaps you could store the others."

The lady said, "Well, you said you did not do very much. In this world, we all can make a contribution by doing little things. When we all do a little...it works. Without you, I would not be looking at this plant and hearing your story of what might be ahead for us all. What is your name young man?"

Ben gulped. "Ben Miller," he said.

"Well, Ben, if what you tell me is true, and if it is truely possible that this plant can deliver the secret to defeat this virus, then you will all be heroes."

"Yes," said Josh, excitedly. "We live in Balloch, at the bottom of the Loch Lomond".

She said, "I know Loch Lomond. Indeed, Josh you are close to the historic town that used to be the capital of the ancient kingdom of Strathclyde, the town of Dumbarton.

The lady thought for a moment. "I could honour you all by giving you a title.

Ben thought the old Morris Minor might be a better option but said nothing.

"So," continued the lady, "starting with the oldest. Your name?"

"Ben," said Ben.

"You would be known as the Earl of Drumtartan. Sorry, the Earl of Dumbarton." She then paused and said "No, that would not be right, if your prophecy is right then you would need a much more heroic title. You need to be knights. So, you Ben would be Sir Ben of Balloch, Knight of the Order of the Bath. How does that sound?"

Ben did not answer but bowed in a most extravagant fashion, a bit unsure as to whether he would now have to take a bath instead of a shower.

"And you, young sir," she said to Josh. "Tell me about yourself".

"My name is Josh," he said, "I love football and play for the Partick Thistle Youth Academy."

"Well you would be known as Sir Josh of Partick, Knight of the Order of the Thistle.

"And young Lady," she said, nodding in Rowan's direction.

"My name is Rowan and I live in a little village called Cardross in a house called Kirkton Byre because our house used to be a farm at one time."

"Well, Rowan." said the lady. "I loved your curtsy when we met. I can't make you a knight. That title is reserved for boys but you would be known as Princess Rowan of Kirkton. (Honorary Knight of the Garter)."

Rowan smiled and wondered what a garter was. She gave another little curtsy.

"And you, young sir."

"I'm Jake," said Jake.

"You are the youngest and sometimes it is hard being the youngest but you too have played your part, what would we call you?"

Jake spoke and told the lady that near their house was an old ruined castle called Darleith.

Her face lit up and she smiled again and said, "Perfect. You would then be known Sir Jake of Darleith, Knight of the order of St Patrick."

Jake had no clue who Patrick was. One of his grandfathers was a minister. He probably knew about saints and stuff.

"I thank you for all you have done, but remember it is the little things that matter. Believe in yourselves and, who knows, you might become a prince, a princess, an earl or even a knight. However, Titles don't matter. What does mater is that you work hard and don't let anyone down."

Gypsy made a little neighing sound.

"Oh...I have missed someone though, haven't I?" she said turning and looking at Gypsy.

"You, too, Gypsy. I can't give you a title but I will never forget you. I have never met a talking horse never mind one that can fly. There was one once but that was long ago. That horse was called Pegasus. Who knows," she laughed, "You might be related."

"Oh we all have heard of Pegasus," said Rowan, quickly, just in case Gypsy decided to speak again.

"I will think of you all as Heroes. But 'The Knights of Gypsy' does not sound right"

"Maam" said Rowan, "you mentioned Pegasus. That sounds quite grand. Could we be 'The Knights of Pegasus'?"

"Yes, of course," said the lady. She seemed pleased with the idea. With that she turned, rounded up the corgis, gave each of the children a lovely smile and thanked them once again. Then she stopped, looked at the ground, thought for a few seconds and, in a more serious tone said. "If what you tell me is true then life for all of us might be difficult.

Things will change, we might need to adapt and if that happens, I will ask you to be as helpful as you can to your mums and dads.

It is sometimes difficult being a parent. Sometimes they may seem to be hard on you, sometimes even unfair, but trust them. Just trust them."

As she turned, she promised she would keep their secret and with one final wave she rounded up the corgis and walked back to the castle.

All four looked at each other and Rowan said, "Is this a dream. Was that real?"

For once, they were all dumbstruck.

Gypsy nudged Rowan and they all climbed on to her back and held on tight. Then, in what seemed like minutes later, Ben and Josh were jumping down and waving goodbye to their cousins.

Ben started cutting the grass at Gran Joan's again and Josh began strimming the edges.

From the house Gran Joan shouted... "Do you want anything to drink?"

"No we are fine" Josh replied.

Shortly afterwards, their dad appeared and praised them for their work.

Gran Joan came to the back door and said, "Thank you both for all you have done tonight. You are wonderful boys. The garden is looking perfect!"

They smiled, looked at each other and under their breath said, "Imagine what she would say if she knew what happened tonight."

Gran Joan smiled as she watched them leaving, feeling strangely proud, though she did not know why.

She turned back into the house, paused and raising her voice. "Ian, can you hear me?"

From his little office, the voice of her husband said, "Yes."

"I have been thinking," she said.

"Sounds dangerous," he replied.

"No seriously" she said, "Living here, so near the Loch, in this community that has been so good to us...with our family and *those four grandchildren*. Are they not just the icing on the cake?"

She was sure she heard, just barely above the clatter of the computer keyboard, a grunt of agreement.

She smiled to herself and the feeling of being somehow blessed!

At the same time Rowan and Jake were removing the saddle and the bridle from Gypsy. Then they walked up to replace them in the stable, just in time to hear their mum shouting it was time for them to be home.

"Have you had fun?" she asked.

"Have we had fun?" Rowan asked.

Jake, with the biggest smile imaginable, nodded, winked and said in a whisper to his sister - "The Knights of Pegasus... Sounds good, doesn't it?"

The *real* Rowan and Jake on Pegasus (Gypsy) with Josh
and Ben beside...

Ross Priory

Rowan and Ben beside the Gunnera plant...

Uncle Jake, Josh and Ben beside that 1932 Morris Minor

Other Children's titles from Neetah Books...

Windscape – by Paul Murdoch

Nominated for the Grampian Children's, Book Award, this is the first of the Jenny and Pavel Adventures. A proposed wind farm on a lonely Scottish island starts a series of events that leads 10-year-old Jenny MacLeod on a dangerous adventure with her friend Pavel. Can she save her father's farm and everything she holds dear, or will the scheming Wildings win the day? *A look at the pros and cons of wind farms through a fast-paced children's adventure.*

The Egg Thief – by Paul Murdoch

The follow up to Windscape, Jenny and Pavel are caught up in an exciting adventure on the western isles of Scotland. While caretaking her uncle's farm on the island of Barra, Jenny and Pavel are embroiled in a plot to steal some very precious sea eagle eggs from the cliffs of Mull. *A look at conservation issues and other cultures through a fast-paced children's adventure.*

Available at www.neetahbooks.com

Visit www.paulmurdoch.co.uk - author visits or on-line talks available with Scottish Book Trust Funding

Lightning Source UK Ltd.
Milton Keynes UK
UKHW010630190920
370179UK00001B/53